SMOUT
& THE LIGHTHOUSE

A Story of Robert Louis Stevenson

Jane Yolen and John Patrick Pazdziora
illustrated by Lyndsay Roberts Rayne

Albert Whitman & Company
Chicago, Illinois

Smout trudges behind his father up the hillside
as the North Sea hisses over the island's rocky beach.
Grey mist whispers stories of adventure in the boy's ears:
stories about sailors, smugglers, pirates.

The Isle of May lighthouse
stands on the hilltop like a castle from a fairy tale,
with its tower and its light
warning ships away from dangerous waters.

Thomas Stevenson looks down at his son.
"Keep up, Smout!" he says.
"This is a lighthouse your grandfather built."

It's the fourth lighthouse they've visited this summer,
each one built by Smout's father or grandfather
or great-grandfather, or an uncle.
Whenever Smout smells saltwater or hears waves,
he knows he isn't far from a lighthouse
built by someone in his family, the "Lighthouse Stevensons".

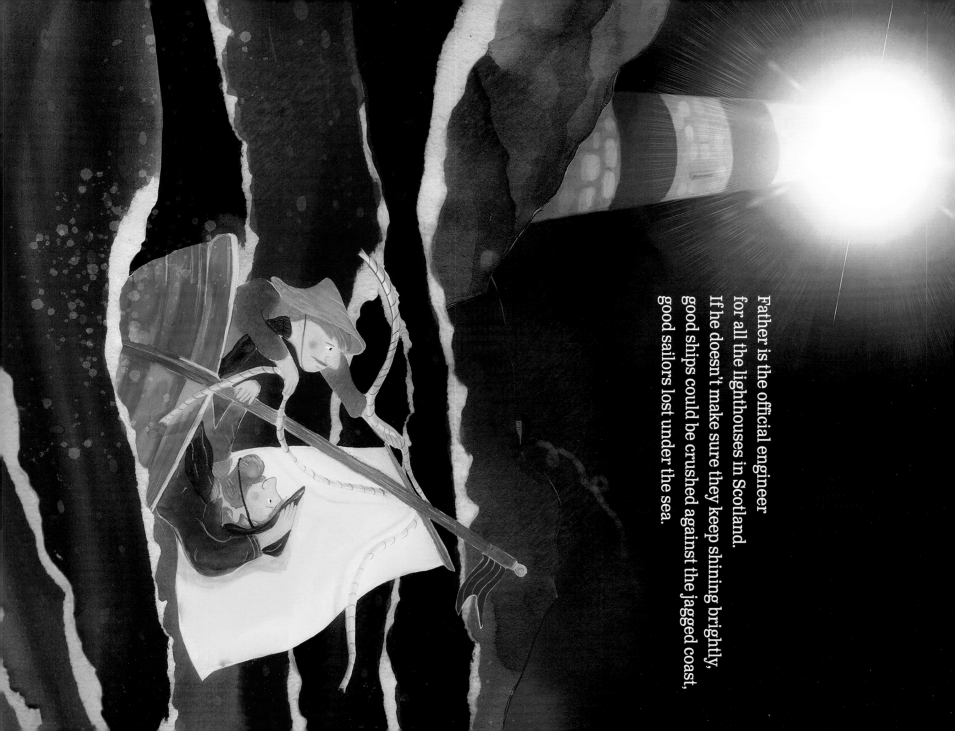

Father is the official engineer
for all the lighthouses in Scotland.
If he doesn't make sure they keep shining brightly,
good ships could be crushed against the jagged coast,
good sailors lost under the sea.

Smout's family expects him
to become a lighthouse engineer,
like his father and grandfather and great-grandfather.

But Smout wants to write stories
His mind is crowded
with tales of faraway cities, strange tropical seas.
It is filled with giants and knights in armor,
hidden treasure, and pirates.
Definitely pirates!

Smout doesn't dare tell Father.
Father can be very fierce.
Just the month before,
he and his father had visited
the St. Andrews lighthouse.
The tower had a cloudy brass railing
and a scratched light reflector.

Father had shouted at the lighthouse keeper
while the poor man nearly drowned in perspiration,
saying, "If a light is not more than middling good,
it will be radically bad.
Ships could be wrecked. Lives could be lost."

Suddenly Smout realizes
Father is talking to him, here and now.

"Keep up, Louis!
Lighthouse Stevensons do not dawdle."

The use of Smout's real name instead of his nickname means Father is losing patience.
So Louis runs forward and puts his hand in Father's.
Like a small boat in the wake of a tall ship,
Smout bobs after Father.
And he tries… he really tries… to keep up.

But all the while Smout thinks about the ships
wrecked against hidden reefs,
torn apart by stormy water.
As he thinks, a story begins in his head...

Storm winds beat the waves to a frenzy.
The ship ran hard against the rocks, and broke and sank.
But the cabin boy washes on to the shore, wet as a ship's rat,
more dead than alive...

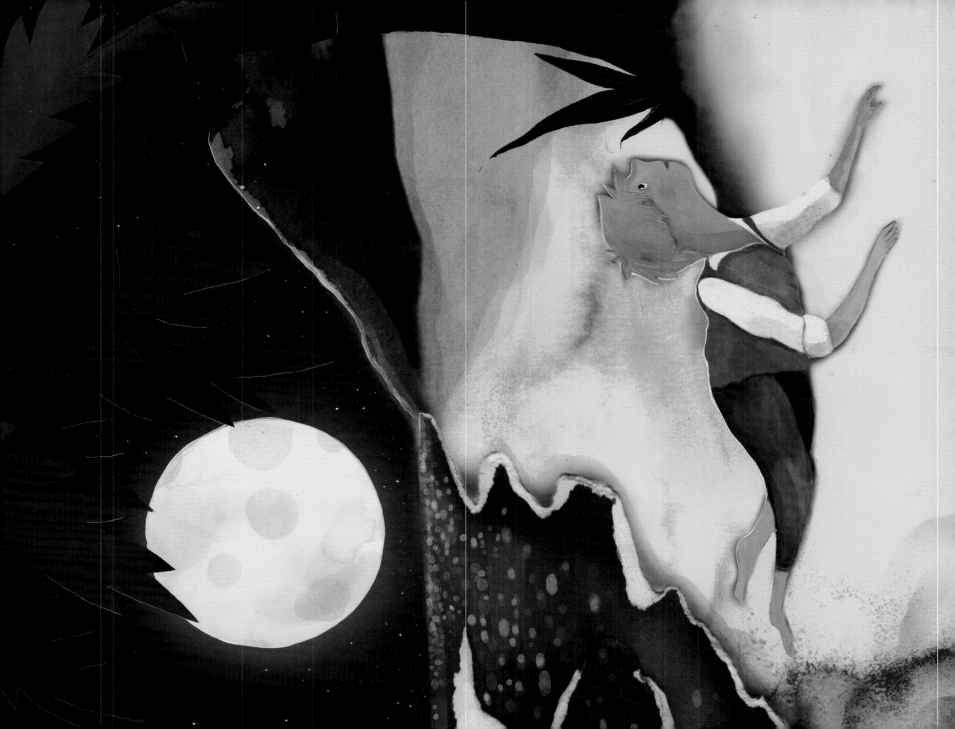

Smout drops his father's hand.
He no longer keeps up.
His steps grow slower.

His mind floods with stories.
He can almost hear the ship breaking…

He can almost see the cabin boy swimming…
He can almost….

The cabin boy lived alone on the island for months.
He pulled handfuls of shellfish from tide pools,
slurping them raw from their shells.
He caught silver fish, more useful than silver coins.
His clothes grew ragged and torn.

Grandfather's lighthouse looms above them—
tall, upright, stern. Like Grandfather. Like Father.
The lighthouse keepers stand at attention
to welcome them.

"Now then, Louis, look there."
Father points to the sea below.
"Lighthouse Stevensons need to be able to read the sea.
Watching the waves will tell you everything you should know
about the coastline.
How many waves run over the reef in a half-minute?
Count them while I speak to the keepers."

Father walks into the lighthouse.

Smout sits down on the cold, damp stone and tries to count waves.

"One, two, three..." he whispers to himself, "nineteen, twenty..."

Or is it seventeen, eighteen?

He has already lost count.

His story is much more interesting than the waves.

Every day, the cabin boy climbed to the hilltop to stare over the bright water until his eyes ached, wondering if he would ever get home. But when at last he saw a ship, it had red sails and a black flag—

PIRATES!

"So, how many waves in the half minute?"
Father has finished with the keepers.
He stands above Smout, holding his pocket watch.

Smout stares hopelessly at the waves. "Nineteen?"

"No!" Father sounds fierce now.
He points again. "Louis, see that big wave?
Follow it—use the eyes God has given you.
Watch it break on that rock.
Now, if you were to use Mr. Nobel's dynamite on
that boulder, what would happen?"

"I don't know," Smout whispers.
He really doesn't know.

"You should know, Louis," Father says.
"A Lighthouse Stevenson needs to know."

Smout's nose has begun to run.
He wipes it on the sleeve of his sweater.

Father sighs.
He reaches into his pocket,
handing Smout a clean, white handkerchief.

"Smout," he says, "If you don't know these things,
how will you ever build lighthouses?
I'm trying to teach you—just as my father taught me."

Smout stares at his tall, strong-faced, fearless father.
The long shadow of the lighthouse covers them.
He feels like the cabin boy
staring at the pirate captain.

He blurts out: "Didn't...didn't grandfather ever tell you any
stories about pirates?"

"About pirates?" Father looks up at grandfather's lighthouse.
Then he looks back at Smout,
who is clutching the now grubby handkerchief.

Father sighs, sits down on the grass.
Something like a friendly silence
suddenly lies between them.

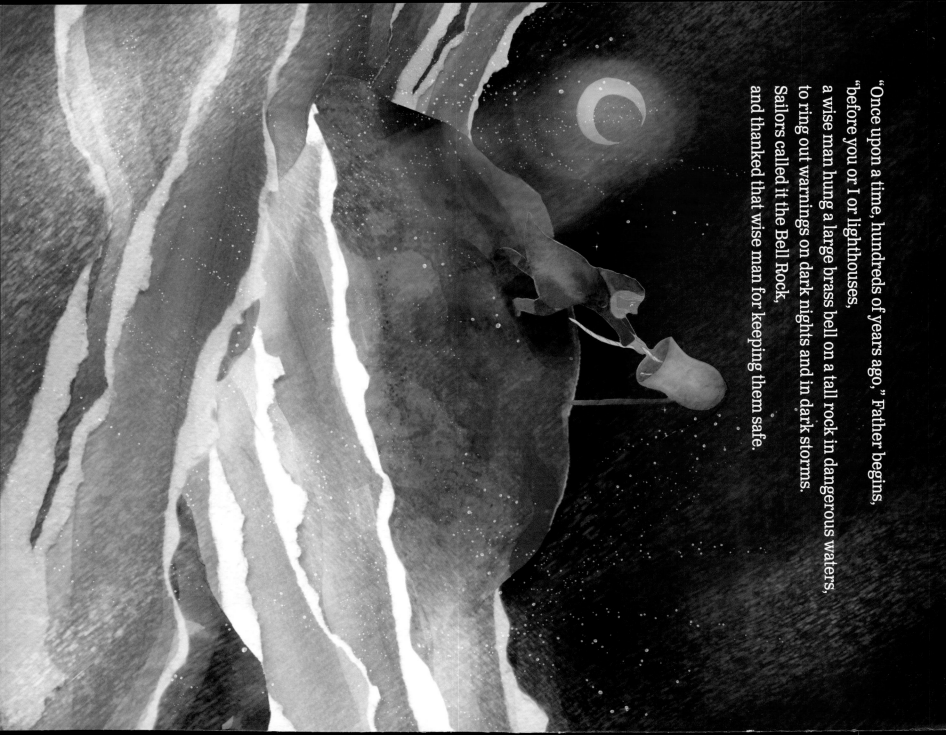

"Once upon a time, hundreds of years ago," Father begins,
"before you or I or lighthouses,
a wise man hung a large brass bell on a tall rock in dangerous waters,
to ring out warnings on dark nights and in dark storms.
Sailors called it the Bell Rock,
and thanked that wise man for keeping them safe.

One dark night, a ship with black sails drew alongside the rock.

A pirate ship! With the dread Sir Ralph the Rover as captain.

He wanted the fine brass bell for himself.

So he leaned out from his ship and cut down the bell.

The pirates sailed away with the bell below deck.

"That very night, a terrible storm spread along the coast. The pirates were blown off course, back to the tall rock, but there was no bell to warn them.

The pirate ship struck the Bell Rock with a terrible crash.
Below deck, the bell tolled once,
and the pirate ship sank beneath the sea with all her crew."

"Truly, Father?" Smout asks.
Father nods. "Truly.
But the waters around Bell Rock
are safe now—all because your grandfather
built a fine lighthouse where the brass bell had hung."

Smout slips his thin hand into Father's strong one.
"I want to write stories like that!
Stories about pirates.
And lighthouses," he added.

Father smiles.
"So did I, when I was your age.
And I still love stories.
But Louis—at least try to learn
about lighthouses.
You are a Stevenson, you know."

"I know, Father," says Smout.
"And I will try."

Then the pirate captain and the cabin boy
walked down the long hill to the shore together,
where their boat waited,
rocking on the uncountable waves.

Biographical Note

Robert Louis Stevenson (1850–1894) came from a family of engineers. His grandfather Robert, father Thomas, uncles, and cousins designed bridges, railways, and major roads but were most famous for their lighthouses. Stevenson Lighthouses stood tall along rocky coastlines and islands throughout the Atlantic and the Pacific Oceans. "Whenever I smell salt water," Louis wrote, "I know I am not far from one of the works of my ancestors."

The Stevensons created lighting technologies that made lighthouses shine brighter and keep ships safer. They found ways to keep lighthouses in Japan standing during earthquakes. They regularly inspected the Scottish lighthouses. It was hard, important work.

Thomas Stevenson wanted his only child to be a lighthouse engineer, too. But little Louis (nicknamed Smout) never did well at school and was often too sick to attend. So, Thomas took him on a lighthouse inspection of Fife, in east Scotland, to strengthen his health in the brisk ocean breeze.

Louis loved the sea and enjoyed walking with his father in "the sunshine, the thrilling seaside air, the wash of waves on the sea-face." But mostly he wanted to write stories: "I loved the art of words and the appearances of life." He wrote his first story when he was six years old, dictating it to his mother, and dreamed of becoming a great author. Even on lighthouse inspections, he made up stories, writing late into the night as moths flapped around his candle.

Thomas was disappointed when he realized that his son would never be an engineer. He tried to convince him to become a lawyer, but gradually his disappointment turned to pride as he read Louis's stories and recognized his son's extraordinary talent with words. In time, Louis became famous for writing essays and travelogues such as *Travels with a Donkey* (1879), books for children including *A Child's Garden of Verses* (1885), and spooky horror fiction like *Strange Case of Dr Jekyll and Mr Hyde* (1886).

In 1881, Louis visited his parents in Scotland with his wife and stepson. On a rainy day, he began doodling pictures to keep them amused. He drew a jagged, rocky coastline, the curve of a deep bay, lines for waves and ocean currents, safe harbors under the mountains. It became a map of an imaginary island—Treasure Island. Soon he was making up a story about the island, the treasure hidden there, and the pirates who came to find it.

He read the story aloud to his family, and his stepson and father loved it. Louis later recalled, "I had counted on one boy; I found I had two in my audience." Thomas offered suggestions and ideas about *Treasure Island*. He invented the list of secret oddments hidden in the dead man's chest and thought of the name for the pirate captain's treasure ship: "The Walrus." *Treasure Island* became the most successful and beloved of all Stevenson's books.

Today, the Stevenson Lighthouses still work to keep the coasts safe in Scotland, New Zealand, Newfoundland, and Japan. And Robert Louis Stevenson's stories are still read and enjoyed as books, audiobooks, musicals, and movies, in dozens of languages all around the world.

To read more about Robert Louis Stevenson, his books, and his family, visit http://robert-louis-stevenson.org.

Robert Louis Stevenson Lighthouses

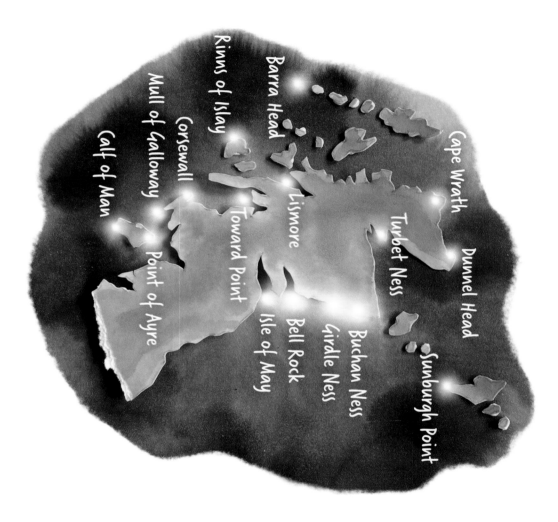

Cape Wrath

Dunnel Head

Rinns of Islay

Barra Head

Turbet Ness

Sunburgh Point

Calf of Man

Mull of Galloway

Corsewall

Lismore

Toward Point

Point of Ayre

Buchan Ness

Girdle Ness

Bell Rock

Isle of May

For Curious Readers

The Bottle Imp, illustrated by Jacqueline Mair

Kidnapped, edited by Barry Menikoff

Treasure Island, illustrated by Mervyn Peake

And in these books, you can start learning more about Stevenson's life and the stories he wrote:

Gherman, Beverley, *Robert Louis Stevenson: Teller of Tales.*

MacLachlan, Christopher, *Robert Louis Stevenson's Treasure Island*, Kidnapped *and* Catriona

For JPP, who happily joined me in the adventure—JY

For Robbie, a story from the sea—JPP

For Ed, with all my love—LRR

Library of Congress Cataloging-in-Publication data
is on file with the publisher.

Text copyright © 2023 by Jane Yolen and John Patrick Pazdziora
Illustrations copyright © 2023 by Albert Whitman & Company
Illustrations by Lyndsay Roberts Rayne
First published in the United States of America in 2023
by Albert Whitman & Company
ISBN 978-0-8075-7484-3 (hardcover)
ISBN 978-0-8075-7485-0 (ebook)

Printed in China

10 9 8 7 6 5 4 3 2 1 CJ 28 27 26 25 24 23

Design by Rick DeMonico

For more information about Albert Whitman & Company,
visit our website at www.albertwhitman.com.

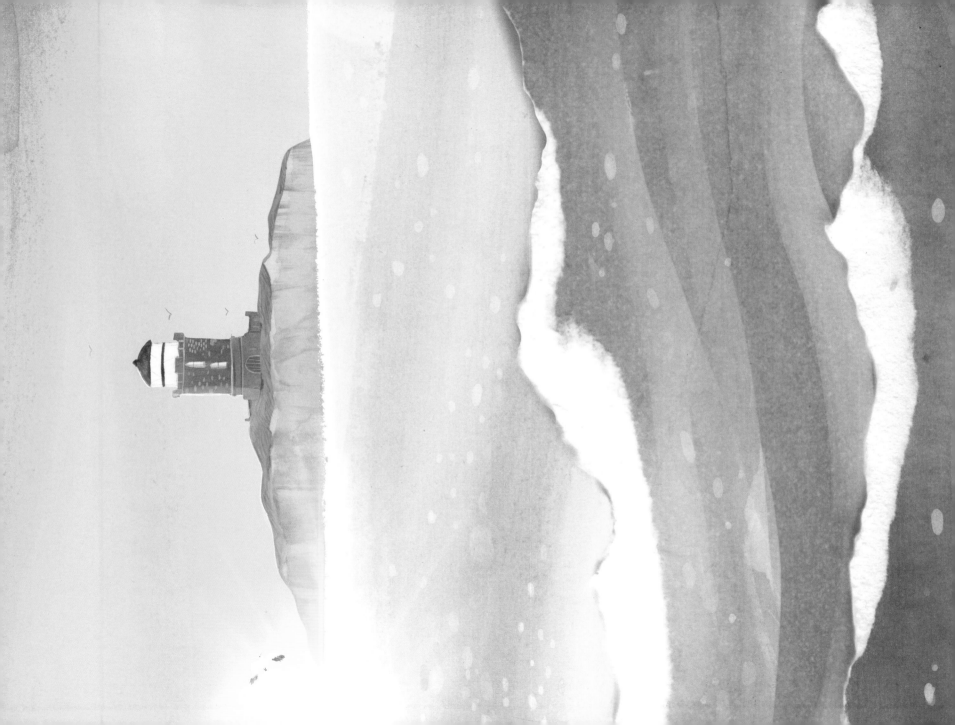

Smout: Scottish nickname for a child or small person

To Betsy and Adam, who raised a powerful writer

—JY

To Shifu/Sensei Koré Grate, artist, warrior, and teacher

—AS

For Lyle, Ellie, and Bodhi

—JL

Text copyright © 2023 Jane Yolen and Ariel Stemple
Illustrations copyright © 2023 John Ledda

Published in 2023 by Beaming Books, an imprint of 1517 Media. All rights reserved.
No part of this book may be reproduced without the written permission of the publisher.
Email copyright@1517.media. Printed in China.

"Karate Kid" poem copyright © 1996 by Jane Yolen, originally published in Opening Days: Sports Poems (Harcourt)

Cover Design: Daniel Cantada

29 28 27 26 25 24 23   1 2 3 4 5 6 7 8 9

Hardcover ISBN: 978-1-5064-8563-8
eBook ISBN: 978-1-5064-9458-6

Library of Congress Cataloging-in-Publication Data

Names: Yolen, Jane, author. | Stemple, Ariel, author. | Ledda, John, illustrator.
Title: Kiki kicks / by Jane Yolen and Ariel Stemple ; illustrated by John Ledda.
Description: Minneapolis, MN : Beaming Books, 2023. | Audience: Ages 4-8. | Summary: At her first karate lesson, a young girl named Kiki regains her confidence and strength after being bullied at school.
Identifiers: LCCN 2022051808 (print) | LCCN 2022051809 (ebook) | ISBN 9781506485638 (hardcover) | ISBN 9781506494586 (ebook)
Subjects: CYAC: Karate--Fiction. | Self-confidence--Fiction. | Bullies and bullying--Fiction. | LCGFT: Picture books.
Classification: LCC PZ7.Y78 Ki 2023 (print) | LCC PZ7.Y78 (ebook) | DDC [E]--dc23
LC record available at https://lccn.loc.gov/2022051808
LC ebook record available at https://lccn.loc.gov/2022051809

VN0003466; 9781506485638; MAY2023

Beaming Books
PO Box 1209
Minneapolis, MN 55440-1209
Beamingbooks.com

A NOTE FROM ARIEL STEMPLE

Being bullied as a kid made it difficult for me to enjoy my hobbies, feel confident, and connect with other people. Despite the support of my family and a few close friends, I felt incredibly alone and scared. When I was seven years old, I started training in a hybrid martial arts style called wu chien pai. The name means "empty space style" in Chinese, and it combines techniques from judo, gung fu, bagua, jujitsu, tai chi, and practical self-defense.

Learning how to do something well made me feel strong. It was an incredibly powerful feeling, especially to an accident-prone kid with depression and anxiety. When someone touches me without permission, I have the strength to free myself from their grasp. I have the courage to stand my ground. When someone tries to use their words or other social techniques to put me down, I have the ability to shield myself from their influence. I have the fortitude to let dismissal drift downstream.

I learned all those valuable life skills from spending my adolescence in a dojo around skilled people who taught me how to hold fast when faced with physical, mental, and spiritual turmoil.

I am a mountain. No one can knock me down.

A NOTE FROM JANE YOLEN

Before there was *Kiki Kicks*, there was the poem. I had written it for a Lee Bennet Hopkins anthology of sports poems. He asked specifically for a poem about karate. Little Ari had been badly bullied in school, and martial arts saved them. I happily agreed. I called the poem "Karate Kid." Ariel was a huge reader and an early writer. And when they were old enough, I asked Ari if they would like to write a picture book with Nana Jane—that's me in the family—about learning to defend themself from bullies. And so, the idea was born. The poem flows parallel to the story and serves as a guiding, empowering inner voice. Ari and I wrote this book together. I hope it is not our last.

In time I will learn to be a mountain like Mama.
For now, I'm proud to be a hill.
A place to start.

I feel strength.
Power.
Peace.

The first lesson is over.
I bow to Sensei.
She smiles.

There is sweat on my forehead.
Little beads of sweat tickle my back.
Sensei says sweating is good.
It's how your body stays safe
while you're getting stronger.

Power.

Sensei shows me a better way.
"Not a mountain yet," she says.
"But a hill.
It is a start."

Peace.

I try to become a mountain like Mama.
My shoulders stiffen.
My hands are claws.

Kick

Mama watches me and nods. Sensei sees it and puts her hand on my shoulder.

"Your mama is a mountain. No one can knock her down."

I want to be strong for the right reasons.
Strong like the older girl.
Strong like Sensei.
Strong like Mama.
Strong like my twin.

Chop.

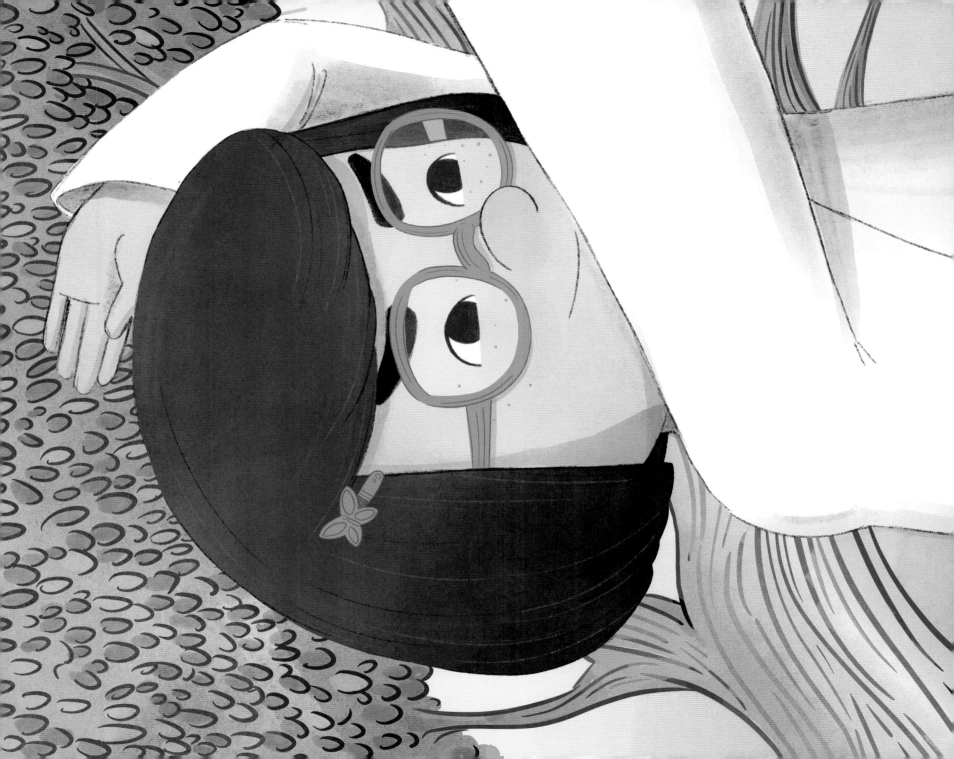

Wind and wave,
Tree and flower.

An older girl shows me how to hold my stances.
How to bend my knees and hold up my guard.
She's bigger than me,
but she doesn't scare me.
She's strong because she wants to be,
working hard to be the horse and the crane.
She's strong for the right reasons.

Dragon left
And leopard right.

Some of the kids at school
are strong without trying.
They use it to hurt people who can't fight back,
just because they can.
They're strong for the wrong reasons.

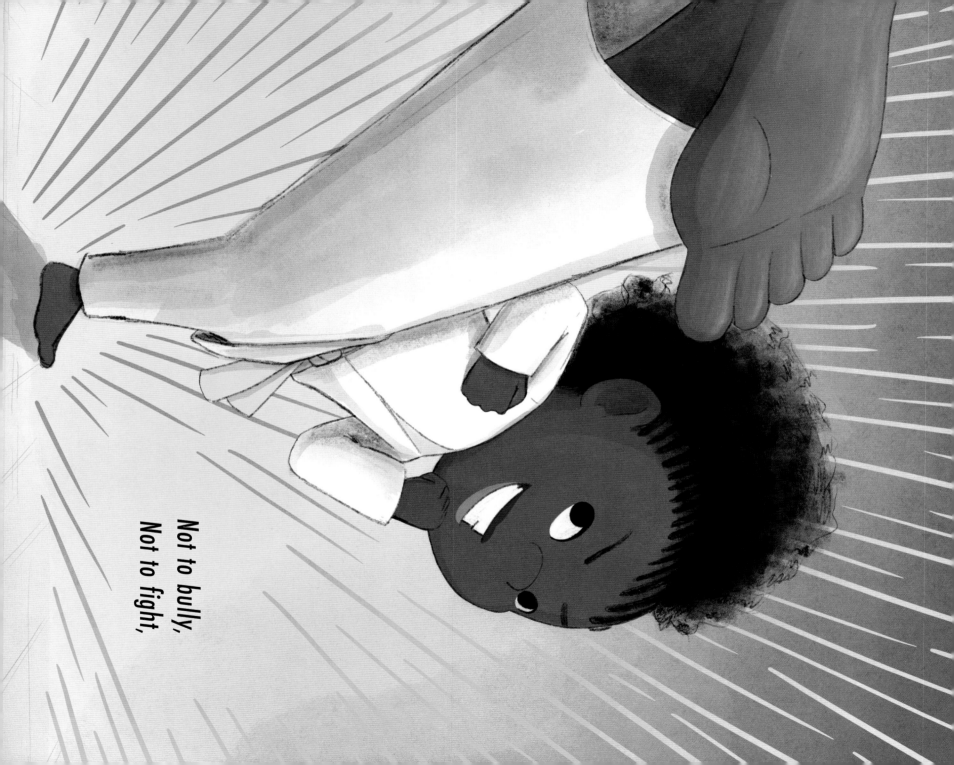

Not to bully,
Not to fight,

I see what Sensei means by a weapon.
The girl to my left is a sword, firm and fast.
She cuts through the air,
and if there was a bully in the place she struck,
he wouldn't be there anymore.

Taught to do
The heart's commands.

I see what Sensei means by gentle.
The boy to my right moves like a river.
He's calm, and he curves before he strikes.

I am elbow,
I am hands

Sensei takes me by the hand.
She shows me how to bow, how to make a fist.
I fold my thumb over my other fingers,
and Sensei pushes my hand against my chest.
"This can be a weapon," she says,
"but it can be gentle too."

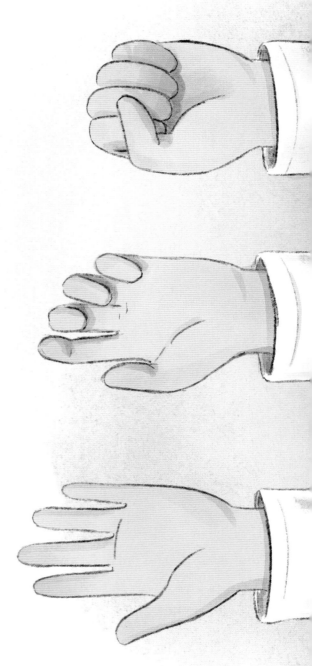

I am flower,
I am knee,

"I am a twin," I say.
"I know," she answers.
"I teach your brother too."
There is a smile in her voice.
I smile back.

I am tiger,
I am tree,

"Kiki," Sensei says,
as if tasting my name.
She smiles.
"In French, Kiki means
Double Happiness."

Training that
I need not fight.

Sensei asks my name.
I answer easily. "Katherine . . .

but my family calls me Kiki."

I am crane
In lofty flight,

Sensei is here to teach,
and the other kids are here to learn.
They're not bullies.
Not like the mean kids at school.
I am learning karate
because of them.

I am wave,
I rise, I fall.

But now I want to learn too.

I walk into the martial arts studio,
Mama by my side.
A tall woman, the sensei,
comes toward us.
She is taller than Mama.
She rolls her shoulders
as she walks.
I am not scared.

My brother started last year. I wasn't ready.

I am wind,
I am wall,

Mama has studied karate
for as long as I can remember.

KIKI KICKS

BY JANE YOLEN AND ARIEL STEMPLE

ILLUSTRATED BY JOHN LEDDA

beaming ☀ books

MINNEAPOLIS